I'm Going To **READ!**™

These levels are meant only as guides;
you and your child can best choose a book that's right.

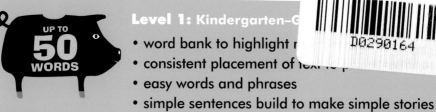

Level 1: Kindergarten–G
- word bank to highlight n
- consistent placement of text to p
- easy words and phrases
- simple sentences build to make simple stories
- art and design help new readers decode text

Level 2: Grade 1 . . . Ages 6–7
- word bank to highlight new words
- rhyming texts introduced
- more difficult words, but vocabulary is still limited
- longer sentences and longer stories
- designed for easy readability

Level 3: Grade 2 . . . Ages 7–8
- richer vocabulary of up to 200 different words
- varied sentence structure
- high-interest stories with longer plots
- designed to promote independent reading

Level 4: Grades 3 and up . . . Ages 8 and up
- richer vocabulary of more than 300 different words
- short chapters, multiple stories, or poems
- more complex plots for the newly independent reader
- emphasis on reading for meaning

For Charles and Elizabeth Claire
Nancy Markham Alberts
1949–2006

LEVEL 3

Library of Congress Cataloging-in-Publication Data Available

2 4 6 8 10 9 7 5 3 1

Published by Sterling Publishing Co., Inc.
387 Park Avenue South, New York, NY 10016
Text © 2007 by Nancy Markham Alberts
Illustrations copyright © 2007 by R. W. Alley
Distributed in Canada by Sterling Publishing
c/o Canadian Manda Group, 165 Dufferin Street
Toronto, Ontario, Canada M6K 3H6
Distributed in the United Kingdom by GMC Distribution Services,
Castle Place, 166 High Street, Lewes, East Sussex, England BN7 1XU
Distributed in Australia by Capricorn Link (Australia) Pty. Ltd.
P.O. Box 704, Windsor, NSW 2756, Australia

I'm Going To Read is a trademark of Sterling Publishing Co., Inc.

Sterling ISBN-13: 978-1-4027-4299-6
Sterling ISBN-10: 1-4027-4299-1

For information about custom editions, special sales, premium and
corporate purchases, please contact Sterling Special Sales
Department at 800-805-5489 or specialsales@sterlingpub.com.

I'm Going To READ!™

JOSELINA PIGGY GOES OUT

Story by Nancy Markham Alberts
Pictures by R. W. Alley

Sterling Publishing Co., Inc.
New York

Joselina hears the birds
and sings a piggy song.

She runs a-zoom a-zoom a-zoom
into her piggy papa's room.

BUT—
Big Pig Papa sleeps.
Too long!

Joselina jumps on him

and kisses his big snout.

She says into his piggy ear,
"Time to go now, Papa dear."

BUT—
Big Pig Papa says,
"No. Too dark."

Joselina shines a light.
Papa jumps up from the bed.

Joselina turns a pirouette
and asks, "Papa, are you set?"

BUT—
Big Pig Papa says,
"No. Too cold."

Joselina gets a scarf,
long and wide and papa-sized.

She wraps her papa like an owl.
"Let's go out. You're warmer now."

BUT—
Big Pig Papa says,
"No. Too stormy."

Thunder rumbles all around.
Joselina Piggy runs.
She makes her piggy papa snug
with a snuggly, piggly hug.

THEN—
Joselina Piggy hugs
her Big Pig Papa.
Too scared.

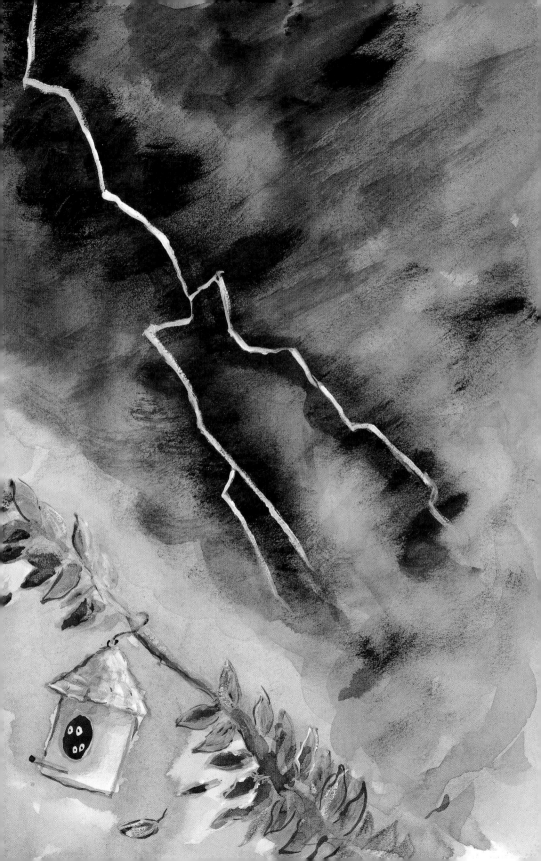

Thunder rumbles go away.
Raindrops start to fall.
Joselina begs on knees,
"Can we go now, piggy please?"

BUT—
Big Pig Papa frowns.
"No. Too wet."

Joselina gets his boots.
She gets his raincoat, too.
She dresses Papa right away.
"See the sun! Let's go, okay?"

BUT—
Big Pig Papa says,
"No. Too hot."

Joselina takes away
raincoat, boots and all.
Big Pig Papa says, "Hi-ho!
That's much better. Off we go!"

BUT—
Joselina Piggy says,
"No. Too hungry."

Joselina eats some toast.
Papa drinks some tea.

Joselina cleans her cup,
then pulls her piggy papa up.

NOW—
out the door
the piggies roar!